THE
MYSTERIOUS
CHEST

AND

OTHER STORIES

**First published in Great Britain by
Amazon UK in 2023**

Text copyright © Dali Ballooni 2023
www.dali-ballooni.co.uk

Illustrations © Olesya Chistyakova 2023

Editor: Louise Swann

ISBN 979-8-3785-5208-5

CONTENTS

THE MYSTERIOUS CHEST

A REMARKABLE STORY ABOUT A PRINCESS
AND MYSTERIOUS CHEST THAT WOULD
FOREVER CHANGE HER LIFE

CHAPTER ONE
Which starts like any other fairytale but quickly turns into a drama.

O nce upon a time in the faraway Kingdom of Tritonia, there lived a Princess named Adelaide. From the day of her birth, she lived in a large royal palace together with her parents, the King and Queen, who surrounded her with their endless love and care.

Indeed, Adelaide's parents loved her so much that they would treat her with presents and all sorts of amazing surprises. By the time Adelaide reached her eighteenth birthday, she had so many presents that it was hard to surprise her with anything else.

Furthermore, for some reason the Princess gradually became more and more withdrawn and often spent time on her own, deep in her thoughts.

Eventually, her parents found it almost impossible to discover presents that would still catch the Princess's attention and make her happy: regardless of whether it was an expensive handbag, a cute puppy or a richly decorated royal carriage, the

Princess would just sigh heavily and pay no interest whatsoever.

As time went by, the King and Queen became very concerned about their daughter. They had no idea what else they could do to make the Princess as happy as she used to be when she was a little child.

However, one day an idea flashed into the King's mind. He decided to entrust four of his bravest and most noble captains with the task of sailing to different parts of the world on a mission to find truly special gifts that could once again bring a smile to the Princess's face.

The very next day, four large and fully equipped ships were ready to set sail in different directions under the command of the four captains.

CHAPTER TWO

Which tells about an extraordinary decision taken by one of the captains.

While the captains of the first three ships immediately set sail to other lands, the Captain of the fourth ship, on the other hand, had a completely different plan.

This Captain knew that he was expected to sail to some faraway country in order to find something unknown. So, after some reflection, he made a decision to put his fate into the hands of destiny.

"I have no idea where we are going to sail to and what exactly we are duty bound to find for the Princess." said the Captain thoughtfully to his sailor-men. "So, I have taken the decision that we simply set sail but do not plot a destination, allowing the ship to travel freely wherever the winds blow!"

Following the Captain's orders, the ship was allowed to sail unchartered, for six days and nights, steered only by nature's powerful winds, sea currents and waves.

It was on the seventh day when the sailors finally saw some unknown land far in the distance.

After dropping the anchor near the shore, the Captain and several of his fellow sailors took a smaller vessel to the shore and then continued their journey of exploration by foot.

They slowly advanced deeper inland until they reached an old forest. It was so overgrown that every step they made was a challenge.

The exploit turned out to be so long and tiring that the Captain himself started doubting his plan to simply follow the road wherever it lead them.

When it seemed that there was no hope left of finding anything at all, the Captain and his men unexpectedly saw an old, slightly crooked, wooden hut, standing in the distance among the tall trees.

"This is our last hope of finding anything at all." thought the Captain to himself.

When they finally reached the hut, the Captain told everyone to wait for him outside. Then, he took a big breath and cautiously knocked on the door.

CHAPTER THREE
Which will certainly raise even more questions without providing any meaningful answers.

Having received no response, the Captain gently opened the creaking door and entered the dark hut.

"I have been waiting for you, Captain," whispered someone's soft mysterious voice.

His attention was instantly drawn to the other side of the room, where he saw a woman, sitting at a round table with her eyes closed, holding a red crystal ball in her hands.

"What you have been searching for is inside the wooden chest on the floor next to you." said the woman with a serene voice. Then, she suddenly opened her eyes and directing her piercing stare at the Captain said, "Please pass this chest to the Princess. Remember that no one else but the Princess is allowed to open it!"

The bewildered Captain just nodded without saying a word. He was completely taken aback by the encounter and the fact that the woman, whoever she was, somehow knew about the Princess and his mission. He took the chest and promptly left the hut.

"We have finally found what we have been looking for. It is time we travel back home!" said the Captain triumphantly to his team.

CHAPTER FOUR
In which Princess Adelaide sees her amazing new gifts.

For six days and nights, the ship sailed through rough seas and steep waves on its return trip to the Tritonia Kingdom.

Upon arrival at the seaport, the Captain saw that the other three ships had already returned from their journeys too.

The King and Queen were delighted to learn that all four captains had returned from their trips safe and sound. Certainly, they also were looking forward to seeing the gifts which they hoped would make their daughter happy again.

Later that day, all four captains arrived at the palace to personally present their gifts to the Princess.

"My Little Adelaide, darling, quickly come downstairs to the Royal Hall to see your new presents!" called the Queen with excited anticipation only to see her daughter sighing and rolling her eyes as she came.

When everyone was finally ready, the King quickly sat next to the Queen and clapped his hands twice to signal his permission for the presentation to begin.

Right at that moment the captain of the first ship entered the Royal Hall. He was followed by three sailors who carefully carried a very large package.

"Your Majesty," started the first captain, "my ship visited many far-away countries and from one of them we have brought the Princess a very special gift - the largest, most beautiful and expensive vase in the world!"

The captain then opened the package to reveal a truly beautiful, richly decorated and certainly large vase.

The Princess briefly glanced at the vase, sighed and then looked away without any interest.

Realising that the first captain's gift failed the challenge, the King quickly clapped his hands twice again and immediately the second captain entered the Royal Hall carrying a small golden cage with a little bird inside.

"Your Majesty, it took a lot of effort to find and bring here this bird from the distant lands of the East. Despite its simple appearance and insignificant size this bird can sing truly amaz...."

But hardly did the Captain manage to finish his sentence, when the bird unexpectedly started singing a wonderful tune.

The King and Queen were so astounded by the bird's remarkable singing that they started clapping excitedly, but only until the moment when they noticed the Princess's disappointed and petulant stare.

"I don't understand. Why is she so critical of everything?" muttered the King with annoyance. He clapped his hands twice again and the third captain entered the Royal Hall accompanied by two sailors carefully carrying a stunning dress.

"Your Majesty, we had to travel far beyond the horizon in order to find and bring back this amazing dress for the Princess. Over one hundred gifted seamstresses worked tirelessly for days and nights. They only used pure golden threads and genuine diamond buttons, as well as the lightest and most expensive silk, in order to create this masterpiece."

Having seen her third present the Princess just closed her eyes and slightly shook her head, as if trying to wake up from a boring dream.

The King felt that it was a complete disaster.

CHAPTER FIVE

Which finally reveals the contents of the wooden chest.

After the complete failure with the first three presents, the King and Queen both looked very sad, tired and miserable. So much effort and all for nothing!

"Reveal the last present," ordered the King with a quiet, hopeless voice.

The fourth Captain slowly entered the Royal Hall, carrying the wooden chest.

"So, what gift have you brought for my daughter?" asked the King miserably.

The Captain looked nervous and appeared lost for words. He gulped some air and started hesitantly.

"Your Majesty, I let my ship sail wherever the winds and waves took her for six days and nights. The gift that my sailors and I eventually found for the Princess is inside this chest. However, I must be honest, I have NO idea what's inside it."

"What? Is this a joke? Get out of my sight immediately!" shouted the King angrily.

The fourth Captain hung his head and was about to leave in shame when suddenly he heard the soft voice of the Princess behind him.

"Wait! Open the chest. I will see what you have brought for me!"

However, instead of enthusiastically opening the chest, to everyone's surprise, the Captain just shook his head.

"Princess Adelaide, with all due respect, I received this chest with the condition that no one but you can open it."

The Captain's unexpected response caused the room to fill with silence and tension. The King's face was slowly turning red with emotion and one could easily tell that he was on the verge of losing control.

Suddenly, the Princess stood up from her chair and came up to the Captain. She gently took the chest and placed it on a table nearby. After a pause, she opened the lid slightly, only to freeze in bewilderment.

"So, what's in there, darling?" asked the King impatiently.

"The chest... is empty," answered the Princess confusedly.

"Scandalous! What a disgrace! How dare you bring an empty chest to my daughter!" shouted the King in anger.

In that moment it seemed things could not get any worse...

CHAPTER SIX
In which the Princess explains it all.

No one had ever seen the King in such a state of fury. His red face and bulging eyes somewhat frightened even the Queen.

"Father, wait!" cried the Princess after completely opening the lid of the chest. "In fact, there is something inside..."

At the bottom of the chest, was a little, hand-written note. The Princess took the note, quietly read it to herself, and then looked back at the chest as if trying to make sense of it all.

"Darling, what does it say?" asked the Queen gently.

"It says: "Dear Princess, please return the chest to me, as most certainly I will need it again. Yours truly, Martha." read the Princess aloud. Suddenly, smiling broadly, she exclaimed delightedly:

"Father, this is truly the best present I could ever receive!"

The King looked from side to side in the hope that somebody could explain to him what exactly was going on.

"But what do you even mean, for heaven's sake? It's just an empty chest!" he yelled, wiping sweat from his forehead.

"Yes, it is indeed empty!" nodded the Princess with a wry smile.

"I truly believe that you have now completely and irreversibly lost me." sighed the King looking into the distance.

"Father, I MUST be frank. You see, I constantly receive all sorts of presents and gifts, and it seems that it must always be something that is the most expensive or the most fashionable! But, as much as I appreciate everything that you and mum have done for me, I am no longer excited by any of those things: thanks to this chest I now know exactly what I have been missing for so long!"

"And may I please, kindly enquire as to what you have been missing for so long?" asked the King rather over-dramatically.

"I have been confined in this royal palace and its grounds for far too long! The best gifts I could ever receive are those of FREEDOM and ADVENTURE!"

"Frankly, young lady, these words do not make any sense to me whatsoever!" yelled the King with authority.

The Princess first lowered her eyes, but then, without saying anything at all, simply ran up to the golden cage that imprisoned the little bird.

After a slight pause, she opened the little door and the bird swiftly flew out of the cage to disappear forever through the wide-open window nearby.

The King sighed with sadness, still trying to make sense of what he had just observed.

"This note, which I must remind you is one of your gifts to me, instructs that I must return it to its rightful owner. This in turn means that I have to travel for six days and nights to the far-away Kingdom. This is the beginning of a real adventure! As a matter of fact, I cannot waste any more time and must get ready for travel immediately. Let the voyage commence!" exclaimed the Princess with shining eyes. Without further ado, she ran away to her room.

"Such behaviour is UNACCEPTABLE!" yelled the King with a broken voice. He was about to follow Adelaide to persuade her to change her mind, but instead stopped short when he felt the Queen's gentle touch on his arm.

"Darling, I think it is time for us to admit that she is no longer a little child." said the Queen with a sad yet resigned voice.

The King turned around and as much as he tried to conceal his tears, his broken voice revealed his emotions.

"Yes, yes... I guess you are right, she is no longer a little child. I have not seen her so happy for a long time. Her happiness is the only thing that matters, isn't it?" asked the King softly.

"Of course it is, darling." quietly responded the Queen.

The King and Queen embraced each other and made a wish in their hearts that their daughter would journey safely and successfully in pursuit of her happiness.

THE END

THE TIMELESS

AN EXTRAORDINARY STORY ABOUT A MAN
WHO GOT HIMSELF INTO A TRULY
PECULIAR SITUATION.

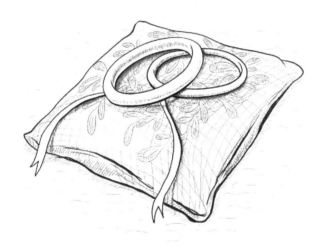

CHAPTER ONE
Which introduces a lonely sad character named Charlie.

In a small town somewhere in England, there lived a man named Charlie. It so happened that Charlie's life was completely unremarkable.

He spent most of his time at work, doing a job that did not provide even the slightest degree of satisfaction, while in the evenings his only company at home was his old dusty television.

In essence, Charlie was a lonely man, who lived a sad life. All of his previous efforts to find a loving companion had failed, so, at some point, he concluded, with a heavy heart, that finding one's true love was an impossible task.

However, his life changed dramatically on one grey autumn morning. On that gloomy day, which did not promise anything other than rain, Charlie went out on his weekly shopping trip.

Passing by the familiar shops on the high street, he was surprised to see that a new shop had popped up amongst the usual ones. Right above its flashy entrance, there was a big red love-heart shaped sign that read: "THE TIMELESS", and right underneath a smaller one: "Find your true love instantly! 100% GUARANTEE!"

The expression on Charlie's face undoubtedly gave away his true feelings about the newly opened business. Shaking his head in disapproval he quickly passed by the shop quietly naming it none other than "ridiculous".

After having visited a couple of stores, Charlie was on his way back home, completely unaware that his ordinary day was about to become quite extraordinary. At first, the dark grey clouds above roared with thunder and then, to Charlie's complete dismay, it started raining heavily.

The rain quickly became so intense that Charlie had no other option but to urgently find shelter in the nearest shop. However, as disappointing as it was for Charlie, that shop turned out to be none other than "THE TIMELESS"...

CHAPTER TWO

In which Charlie meets the owner of the shop.

When Charlie realised - with great disappointment - where he had ended up, his first reaction was to turn around and leave that place immediately.

However, seeing through the shop's large windows the strong rain outside and soaking wet passers-by desperately fleeing to find a shelter of their own, he decided to stay after all.

Suddenly, from behind him, a voice rang out: "Welcome!"

Charlie turned around to see a tall, well-presented gentleman coming downstairs whilst trying to discreetly chase away some white smoke that followed behind him.

"Welcome to "THE TIMELESS!" he again cheerfully greeted the visitor.

"Thank you. To be honest, I am just hiding from the rain. I hope you do not mind. I will of course leave as soon as the weather improves a bit," explained Charlie quickly, hoping to avoid any possible misunderstanding.

"Of course, of course, not to worry. Here we welcome everyone!" responded the man with a big smile. "By the way, my name is Mr Smith and I am an inventor, a businessman and the owner of this humble place."

"My pleasure," replied Charlie with little enthusiasm and still glimpsing outside with hopes that the rain might end any time soon.

"If you do not mind me asking, are you looking to find your true love by any chance?" asked Mr Smith cheerfully, slightly raising his right brow. "You see, our company specialises in finding true love, and we offer a 100% success rate guarantee. I am proud to say that we use only the most reliable and advanced technology!"

Charlie was not in the mood to politely engage in the conversation. The whole situation already felt like a heavy burden upon him, and not having the option of simply walking away forced Charlie to voice his honest opinion about the new business.

"With all due respect, finding true love is not simple and advanced technology has nothing to do with it! You give people false hopes and simply make money from their natural desire to find someone they can love!"

Having expressed his strong views, Charlie yet again threw a hopeful glance through the window.

"Well, I completely understand your concerns." responded the shop's owner with an air of embarrassment. "However, I must emphasise that our technology is much more advanced than you probably think."

"Of course, it is." replied Charlie rolling his eyes dismissively.

Mr Smith gave a dry smile and then politely pointed towards a customer armchair, inviting Charlie to have a seat.

"Well, as far as I can judge, you are stuck here for the time being. Why don't we have a seat and I will tell you a little bit about our company just to fill in some time."

Charlie sighed, and faced with no choice just nodded in response. He left his shopping bags at the entrance door and took a seat in a cosy armchair next to Mr Smith's table.

Meanwhile, the rain outside had no intention of stopping.

CHAPTER THREE

In which Mr Smith something very important to Charlie and then makes an offer that is impossible to reject.

"You see, finding one's true love is a task of unimaginable complexity," started Mr Smith with a solemn voice. "As a matter of fact, one must be very lucky indeed to find the love of their life on the same street or in the town where they live. I believe that the most important question one should ask is NOT what to do if their soul mate is born in another country. Nor is it what to do if they are born on another continent and probably speak a language foreign to you... The MOST important question of all, that each and every individual should ask themselves, is what if their other half is born in a COMPLETELY DIFFERENT TIME?"

Mr Smith's unexpected conclusion made Charlie cough. Having allowed the guest to clear his throat, Mr Smith continued.

"Your true love might have already lived in the past or is yet to be born in the future. Such a possibility is hard to deny! Moreover, the chances that your true love was born in the same time as you, and lives somewhere nearby, is one in a gazillion. And I assure you that these are scientifically proven calculations!" emphasised Mr Smith with the utmost confidence.

It is worth mentioning that Charlie had once had thoughts of a similar kind.

"I am, however, delighted to inform you that not only can our company search and locate your true love within a

town, a country or a continent... but also, using advanced technology exclusively available only to us, we can search within all time layers and dimensions. Using simpler terminology, we conduct a search in the PAST, PRESENT as well as the FUTURE!" proudly, and quite loudly, concluded Mr Smith.

"And the future...?" repeated Charlie just to break the uncomfortable silence.

"Yes, yes, and the future too!" confirmed Mr Smith with all seriousness.

"And just how do you do that?" said Charlie dubiously.

"Well, we use the so-called I.M.C. which stands for Interdimensional Molecular Catapult or, if using vocabulary that is easily understood by the general public, we use a TIME TRAVEL MACHINE."

The silence that followed made the rain pouring outside and the wall-clock ticking inside sound somewhat louder.

"But aren't you concerned that by sending people into

the past or the future, you may change, if not completely destroy, the present?" asked Charlie patronisingly.

"No, not at all. You see, there are numerous parallel universes and our so-called present is just one of many. Therefore, any change in the past will just add a new parallel universe without affecting the times we live in."

Charlie did not quite comprehend the response provided to him, yet to his ear, the explanation sounded quite reasonable.

"So, would you be interested to learn who your true love is?" asked Mr Smith with a mysterious voice.

The question was put so bluntly that any sensible person would have felt that there was only one right way to answer it. Charlie hesitated, but his concerns were instantly settled by Mr Smith's comforting voice:

"The initial information is free of charge and only takes a couple of minutes. Moreover, it does NOT commit you to anything at all."

After the provided reassurance, Charlie felt that he had no choice but to shrug his shoulders and nod in agreement.

CHAPTER FOUR

In which Charlie takes a very important decision which will change his life forever.

Mr Smith opened the table drawer and carefully took out a somewhat unusual device consisting of a red crystal ball on a wooden stand with numerous wires and electric switches attached to it. He carefully placed it on the table in front of Charlie and then switched it on.

"This is an Ultra-Chromosome Scanner - not only is it one of a kind but also exclusively available only to OUR company!" declared Mr Smith proudly. "Please place your right hand palm down on the ball."

Following the instructions, Charlie gently placed his hand on the red ball feeling its warmth when the device started to scan.

"Great! The information will now be transferred into the main computer for a detailed analysis, and then the final in-depth results will be available in a minute or so," stated Mr Smith using a serious voice whilst raising his eyebrows for a greater effect.

Seconds later, the printer under the table started printing out what was apparently the results of the scan.

"Well, well, well," muttered Mr Smith thoughtfully as he read the printout, "this is quite fascinating..."

"What do you mean quite fascinating?" responded Charlie with frustration. "Could it be the fact that your so-called in-depth results barely cover even half the page you are holding?"

"No, not that at all. You see, according to the information provided by the Ultra-Chromosome Scanner, it is clear that you are generally not a very sociable person - rather, someone who loves peace and quiet. These results also indicate your somewhat old-fashioned attitude towards a relationship desiring to find someone whose presence will not burden you and whose quietness will be a song of joy to your ears. As a result, this is the exact type of personality you'd only find in the STONE AGE - loving, yet devoid of any conversation."

Surprisingly, Mr Smith's conclusion suddenly reflected what Charlie had long been looking for - a caring and quiet woman. Unexpectedly, from this point on Charlie became fully drawn into the conversation.

"I would estimate that with our Interdimensional Molecular Catapult time travel to the Stone Age will only take a couple of minutes, in addition to the usual formalities, of course," reflected Mr Smith putting the printout aside.

"And what are the formalities?" enquired Charlie with confusion.

"Well, firstly the financial element would need to be settled and then a no-dispute agreement signed in order to avoid any potential legal confusion, so to speak."

"And would you kindly disclose the cost of the financial element?"

"Well, the total cost of the service is ALL of your assets including property, cash, shares, valuables and all money kept in your bank accounts," calmly responded Mr Smith.

"Surely you are joking!" exclaimed Charlie nervously.

"No, not at all. You see, you will have no other choice but to leave EVERYTHING you owe behind you in this time, as you simply will not be able to take anything along. Even if you could potentially take some money with you on your travel in time, it would still be completely worthless at the destination. I hope you understand."

Charlie was sitting on the edge of the armchair reflecting upon Mr Smith's response.

"But what if something goes wrong?"

"You see, we only use the most reliable and advanced techno..."

"I've already heard that before." interrupted Charlie, "But what if for some reason we do not like each other when I get there? What happens then?"

"I can assure you that you will like each other very much!" responded Mr Smith with a smile full of confidence. He opened the table drawer again and took out a couple of blank forms.

"Please fill these in and sign at the bottom of each one. You can use this pen, should you wish."

Charlie threw himself back in the armchair with a sigh. He felt his head overflowing with thoughts. He glimpsed through the window. It was still raining heavily. What a grey and miserable day, he thought to himself.

This truly extraordinary situation suddenly gave Charlie a little hope that there was a place somewhere far away, in another time, where he could be happy. Indeed, hope and happiness were feelings that he had not felt for a very long time...

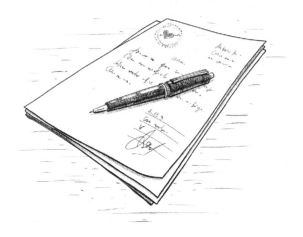

CHAPTER FIVE

In which Charlie finds himself at the point of no return.

"I agree!" Charlie suddenly interrupted his own silence. He promptly took the pen, leaned over the table, and then briefly completed and signed the documents.

Mr Smith took the signed papers and then asked randomly:

"Do you have any fears, by any chance?"

"I do not think so..." responded Charlie thoughtfully. "All I know is that I was scared of wolfs as a child. That's all really."

Mr Smith nodded with understanding and then headed to the room next door.

"Please allow me a couple of minutes. In the meantime, feel free to help yourself with a cup of tea."

However, a cup of tea was the last thing on Charlie's mind. Sitting still, his thoughts were miles away only to be brought back to reality by Mr Smith's cheerful voice.

"I have finally managed to find your size!" he joyfully announced, having returned with a large furry piece of some animal's skin. "Please change, so that we can make sure that it fits you snuggly. Take this too as it is a part of the costume" he added, passing a large Stone Age wooden club over to Charlie.

"Do you mean I should change right now?" muttered Charlie hesitantly.

"Well, I see no reason to waste time, so to speak. Although, of course, it is entirely up to you. Would you rather prefer to make another appointment, say, for tomorrow morning instead?"

After a brief hesitation, Charlie stood up with a face full of determination, and then took the animal skin and club from Mr Smith.

"Where can I change?" he asked somewhat quietly but with a brave expression on his face, to which Mr Smith gallantly responded by pointing towards the room next door.

Minutes later the door opened revealing Charlie in his new outfit with the club in his hands.

"I must say that this Stone Age style suits you really well," commented Mr Smith nodding his head with approval.

"Would you mind, please!" yelled Charlie with embarrassment.

"Of course! I completely understand." retreated Mr Smith politely. "Please now make your way upstairs. You will find our Interdimensional Molecular Catapult on the 1st floor on your left."

Charlie slowly headed towards the stairs whilst adjusting

the rough animal skin on his way and dragging the rather heavy club behind him.

When passing near the entrance door he saw his shopping bags on the floor. He carefully turned to Mr Smith with a question in his eyes.

"I am afraid that you cannot take your shopping bags with you," was the strict answer.

Following the directions, Charlie went upstairs to the first floor and entered a fairly large, empty, windowless room. The ceiling was completely covered with hundreds of bulbs and various electric wires.

"Please take your position right in the centre of the room, indicated by the cross" confidently instructed Mr Smith. "At some point, it will become extremely bright, so I recommend keeping your eyes shut."

Charlie briefly looked around and was about to ask something but quickly realised that by then it was much too late.

Mr Smith closed the heavy metal door, thoughtfully entered some details on a small computer device at the entrance to the Interdimensional Molecular Catapult room and then confidently pressed a red START button underneath.

Charlie was standing in the middle of the room with his eyes closed. He was holding the club with both hands on his chest tightly pressed against the dusty animal fur.

Suddenly, the room became illuminated with hundreds of bright bulbs; white smoke began to fill it until it was impossible to see anything around.

After the lights flashed several times, the smoke started gradually disappearing revealing what was now a completely empty room.

Mr Smith opened the door wide to allow the remaining smoke to escape the room. Standing at the entrance to the Interdimensional Molecular Catapult room, he was deep in his thoughts.

"Stone Age then..." he said quietly to himself.

He might well have kept on thinking about whatever he was thinking about for some time longer if it weren't for the bell ringing on the shop's entrance door. He quickly adjusted his bow tie and rushed downstairs.

"Welcome to "THE TIMELESS"!" cheerfully greeted Mr Smith his next visitor while discreetly chasing away the white smoke that followed behind him...

THE END

The Prince of Caledonia

A SAD STORY WITH A JOYFUL ENDING.

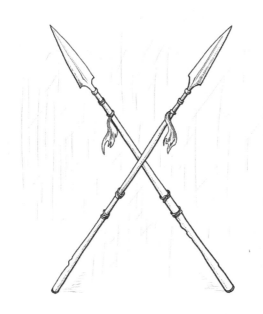

CHAPTER ONE

Which tells about an unhappy Prince Elliott.

Once upon a time, in the Kingdom of Caledonia, there lived an all-powerful wealthy King, his wife, the Queen and their newborn son whom they lovingly named Prince Elliott.

Sadly, from the very birth, the little Prince suffered from a serious ailment which made it difficult for him to find friends. Eventually, he started avoiding the presence of other people altogether, choosing to live a secluded life instead.

When Elliott eventually grew into a fine young man, he would often reflect with great sadness about his ailment which would never allow him to find a Princess who could pay him even the slightest attention, let alone agree to marry him.

It goes without saying that Elliott's parents were tremendously concerned about him. The King offered to pay as much gold as needed to anyone who would be able to cure his son. However, all the best surgeons one after another declared that curing the Prince's ailment was indeed impossible.

Eventually, the King was left with no other choice but to ask for help from a healer whom he had once known well. The Healer was known for her knowledge of mystical matters and nature's secrets.

So, the following day the King and his royal guards set off on a long journey to the place where the Healer lived.

Riding through endless hills and a dark overgrown forest, the King and his men finally reached the old crooked hut in the midst of the woods where the Healer lived.

CHAPTER TWO

Which tells more about the Healer and the King's request for help.

When the Healer heard the sounds of approaching horses and their riders, she came out to greet the unexpected guests.

Recognising the King himself among them, the woman felt anxious, and her heart sank from the sudden rush of old memories. Yet she quickly gathered herself, came up to the King and looking straight into his eyes, greeted him with emotion.

"Good day, Richard. I am very happy to see you again!"

"Good day, Martha," replied the King self-importantly and after a short pause added: "Please address me the way one addresses an all-powerful King. Only my family members may call me Richard."

"I understand." quietly responded the Healer, lowering her eyes."What has made Your Majesty come to this abandoned part of the Kingdom?"

"I have come to ask for assistance. I must talk to you in private."

The Healer invited the King to enter her modest hut. Having made himself comfortable on an old squeaky chair next to the fireplace, the King began his story.

"You are probably aware that quite a few years ago my wife and I were blessed to become parents to our wonderful son. However, our happiness did not last for long: since his birth, my son has been suffering from a serious ailment. When he was a little child he was happy and content despite the difficulties. However, a lot has changed over the years, and he is now a grown-up young man. He has been trying unsuccessfully to find a Princess who would be able to appreciate his good human qualities above his physical problem."

The Healer was listening attentively to the King's story whilst at the same time trying to conceal her sudden anxiety as a result of the words about the Prince's ailment.

"I remember from the times of our childhood friendship," continued the King, "that you have some very special abilities passed on to you by your mother. I have come here in person to kindly ask you to help my son to find a princess who would be worthy of him. I will stop at nothing and will readily pay generously for your service. You are probably my last hope to change anything for the better."

"Your Majesty," responded the Healer somewhat uneasily, "I don't need any money, and I am happy to help you as much as I can without any reward whatsoever."

At that moment the grateful King took her hand and spoke emotionally to her in a quiet trembling voice.

"Martha, if you manage to help my son find a good wife, I will be thankful to you for the rest of my life!"

After their brief conversation, the King bid his farewell and set off with his guards back to the palace.

Although the King tried not to expect much from his meeting with the Healer, he knew perfectly well that she was indeed his LAST hope...

CHAPTER THREE

In which the Healer uses a mysterious red ball to look at the events of the future.

The Healer stood at the window looking thoughtfully at the King and his men fading away into the distance beyond the trees. This unexpected meeting awakened many of her old, and somewhat bitter, memories.

As she contemplated the King's request, she fixed her gaze on a small red crystal ball sitting on a table across the room. She sat down at the table, took the ball in her hands, and began to look attentively directly into its centre: it seemed that by doing so she was somehow able to view images that were only visible to her.

"This is quite interesting... and who would have thought!" she whispered to herself as she put the crystal ball aside.

The Healer then took a piece of paper and quickly scribbled something on it. Then she carefully looked around the room until her gaze fell upon a small, old, wooden chest.

Having placed the note inside, she closed it securely and left the chest on the floor next to the entrance door. The Healer quickly returned to her seat, took up the crystal ball once more and closed her eyes, as if expecting something to happen any moment soon.

Just a few moments later, someone knocked on the hut's door. After a pause the door creaked open revealing someone, dressed as a captain, standing on the doorstep. The man entered hesitantly into the dim room, only to freeze in surprise when he heard the mysterious voice of the Healer from the other side of the room.

"I have been waiting for you, Captain. What you have been searching for is inside the wooden chest on the floor next to you. Please pass this chest to the Princess. Remember that no one but the Princess is allowed to open it!"

One could easily tell that the unexpected guest was he completely bewildered by what had just happened. Yet, quickly gathered himself, nodded in agreement and then picked up the chest and promptly left.

Meanwhile, the Healer remained sitting at her table deep in thought.

"Well, now it is just a matter of patience..." she muttered to herself.

CHAPTER FOUR

In which the Healer meets a Princess who arrives from another Kingdom to return the chest.

Many days had passed since the Healer gave the wooden chest containing the handwritten note to a stranger. One sunny day, someone gently knocked on the old hut's door, and when the Healer opened it, she saw a beautiful young woman on her doorstep.

"Hello!" the young woman greeted with excitement. "I suppose, you are Martha. My name is Adelaide... and I have travelled all the way from another Kingdom to return this to you."

The young woman was holding that very wooden chest.

"Oh, my dear, how glad I am that you have finally arrived," responded the Healer, having recognised the Princess whose image she had seen in the crystal red ball. She took the chest, and looking into the beautiful eyes of the Princess she thanked her for returning it safely.

"I don't know exactly what all this means, but you probably have no idea how much my life has changed thanks to this wooden chest."

"Well, I believe that this is just only the beginning," responded the Healer somewhat mysteriously. She kindly invited the girl to come inside.

With great interest, Adelaide was looking around the Healer's modest, yet cosy hut, which was filled with all sorts of old books and bunches of dried herbs. Everything here seemed so new and infinitely appealing to her.

Finally, having had some rest after her long and tiring trip, Adelaide told the Healer about her journey, which had begun in a faraway kingdom, continued through dangerous seas and endless hills, finally ended in that very overgrown, dark forest.

During their conversation, the Healer briefly mentioned her special abilities revealing that her sending of the handwritten note inside the chest had been for a very special reason.

"Adelaide, I happen to personally know the King of these lands, and I think that he and his family would be delighted to meet you; especially, when they learn that you are a Princess from another kingdom."

Adelaide simply nodded with a big smile and a face full of anticipation.

The Princess felt that it was a completely new chapter in her life: that page after page was filled with exciting turns and twists, and the Healer's proposal was definitely one of them.

CHAPTER FIVE

In which Adelaide meets Prince Elliott and finds out about his lifelong ailment.

The following day, Adelaide and the Healer travelled to the palace. The King and Queen were very pleased to meet the Princess and pleasantly enchanted by her beauty and good nature.

During their conversation, the Queen mentioned to Adelaide that they had a son, Prince Elliott, and cautiously invited the Princess to meet him.

Both the King and Queen did not have the courage to tell Adelaide about their son's ailment, as they were concerned that this might scare her off. Instead, they just briefly mentioned that the Prince preferred privacy to any company.

Later that day, Adelaide finally met the Prince, who was all by himself in the opposite part of the palace. Upon entering his chambers, she saw him standing by the window and gazing far into the distance. When the Prince heard the sound of footsteps, he turned around. At that moment, Adelaide was completely mesmerized by the beauty of his calm and serene face.

"Good day! You are Adelaide, aren't you!" greeted the Prince. "I have been informed that you are a Princess from a faraway Kingdom."

"Good day, Elliott!" she answered with a smile. "Yes, indeed, I have travelled from far and I am only here thanks to some absolutely incredible events!"

While the Princess was telling her story, Elliott listened to her attentively. However, at some point, he suddenly interrupted her in the middle of the sentence.

"You have such an amazing voice: it sounds so beautiful."

The Princess listened to Elliott in slight confusion, and a shy smile remained on her lips until she suddenly realised why the Prince kept talking only about her voice.

Indeed, he was looking at Adelaide, yet at the same time, there was a feeling that his gaze seemed to pass right through her as if she was invisible. The smile finally left her lips when she realized that the Prince was blind.

Adelaide's quietened voice probably gave away her sadness when she realised what exactly Prince Elliott's ailment was. However, quite soon it also became clear that his blindness need not become a barrier, as they simply continued their conversation.

They spent a lot of time together, telling each other about themselves and their families. The Prince was not only an interesting speaker but also had a great sense of humour, often making the Princess laugh at his amusingly imaginative stories.

In the following days they met and talk again and again. Adelaide had a feeling that the Prince, unlike anyone else, understood her desire to be free and happy. As for Elliott, although he could not physically see the Princess, he liked her voice and enjoyed the fulfilling conversations they had. Undoubtedly, he was very happy that, despite his ailment, she still seemed to take a genuine interest in him.

The King and Queen were extremely happy that Elliott readily spent his time with the Princess, and they were grateful to see him as cheerful and sociable as they had once known him when he was a little child.

The King personally thanked the Healer for her tremendous help, and despite his numerous attempts to reward her generously, she categorically refused. Instead, for some unknown reason, she asked the King for his forgiveness and expressed genuine regret for not being able to help earlier...

CHAPTER SIX

In which Adelaide witnesses a truly heartbreaking scene.

Time flew fast, and a few months later the King and Queen were absolutely thrilled when Elliott and Adelaide announced their engagement.

A decision was taken that the couple would marry on the first day of summer and that the whole Kingdom would be invited along to celebrate this wonderful occasion.

However, as often happens in life, sometimes just one event can change the course of the story.

One day, Adelaide was passing by the Royal Library when through the wide-open doors she saw Prince Elliott in the distance. He was slowly walking along the library shelves, barely touching neatly arranged books with his fingertips.

Suddenly he stopped, took one of the books and opened it as if intending to read it. After slowly flipping a few random pages, he unexpectedly stopped and a moment later threw the book angrily on the floor. Tears rolled down his sad face.

Without revealing her presence, Adelaide quickly returned to her chambers. She lay down on her bed and cried bitterly. The mere thought of Elliott's painful suffering because of his inability both to read books and see the world around him, plunged her into despair. Adelaide spent the following night in tears thinking about how, if at all, she could help the man she loved so dearly.

Unable to fall asleep, and although exhausted from her endless thoughts, all of a sudden an idea came to her mind. Adelaide remembered about the Healer and wondered if she somehow would be able to help the Prince.

Without delay, she quickly got dressed and set off under the cover of darkness on the long journey to the Healer's old hut.

CHAPTER SEVEN
Which reveals a terrible truth about the Healer's past.

After a long and tiring journey, the Princess was glad to finally reach the familiar hut. With tears in her eyes, Adelaide told the Healer about the upsetting scene that she had witnessed the day before, and begged her to do something to help Prince Elliott.

"Please do something! I'm ready to make any sacrifice for his happiness!" pleaded Adelaide.

"Darling, I see how much you love him but there is nothing that I..."

The Healer suddenly stopped and looked uncertain whether to continue. She then lowered her eyes and continued with a quieter voice.

"Adelaide, I must confess to you something very important. Apparently, it is... It is MY fault that the Prince was born blind. I think... I managed to put a curse on him before he was even born."

"A curse? Why would you do such a thing?!" exclaimed the horrified Princess, feeling her own heartbeat. "Could you really have done something so terrible?"

"It is a long and sad story. Maybe one day I'll tell it to you. I guess, sooner or later, one pays for the mistakes of the past, and now it is the time to pay for mine."

"I do not understand," whispered the Princess wiping her tears away.

"Darling, please listen carefully," said the Healer emotionally. "You see, the curse is only powerful if the person who is cursed is not aware of it. The only way it can be lifted from the Prince is if I myself tell him about it. When the Prince learns about the curse and acknowledges its presence then within days it will completely lose its power, allowing the Prince to see."

"Then we must hurry up! The Prince must know immediately!" exclaimed Adelaide jumping to her feet. "Let's head to the palace at once!"

"Not so fast! I am afraid I need to get ready first. I assure you, the King will be furious when he finds out the truth."

"No, no, he will be happy for Elliott! He will forgive you!"

"Adelaide, darling, you cannot yet imagine just how full of sorrow a parent's heart can be. When the King learns the truth, he will never forgive me. I need time until tomorrow. Now I must collect some of my possessions and be ready to leave this place... forever."

CHAPTER EIGHT
Which proves that not all stories end equally well.

The Healer kept her word and went to the Royal Palace in the morning of the following day. In the beautifully ornate room of the Royal Hall, in the presence of the King, the Queen and Adelaide, with a trembling voice, she personally told Prince Elliott about the curse she had put on him long before his birth.

The Healer assured the Prince that the curse would fade away within a few days and he would eventually gain the ability to see.

Without trying to explain the reason for the curse and her actions, the Healer only said that she was much too young at the time and her heart was filled with hatred and that, of course, she had no forgiveness for what she had done to him.

Having heard all this, the Prince was overwhelmed with happiness. He could have not even contemplated that one day he would have the ability to see. The Princess hugged him with devotion; she too was full of joy.

The Queen was looking at the young couple with a sad smile, shaking her head in disbelief and repeating:

"Oh, how glad I am for both of you!"

Only the King sat in silence. Listening to the Healer, he seemed to freeze in disbelief. Right before his eyes flashed the day when the Prince was born and how happy the young parents were to see their newborn.

He also vividly remembered that feeling of horror when days later they realized that the baby was blind. How worried were they about him and his future all these years, shedding bitter tears every other night...

All those thoughts and memories made the King's eyes red with rage. Suddenly, as if awakened from a terrible dream, he began to call for the Royal Guards.

"Arrest her! Arrest the witch! Lock her up!"

The King was not yet aware that the Healer had left the palace in a rush. When he found out about the escape, he ordered the royal guards to immediately head to the dark forest where her old, crooked, hut stood.

However, they failed to find anyone there either, and the hut's wide open door was yet another sign that its owner had no intention of returning.

The Healer's escape filled the King with anger and frustration and made him even more determined to do everything possible to have her captured.

He ordered the Royal Guards to continue searching all over the Caledonia Kingdom and offered a generous reward to anyone who could find her.

Meanwhile, a few months later, the Prince and Princess got married on the first day of summer, just as they had planned.

On that day, for the first time in many years, the King and Queen felt their hearts full of warmth and contentment. It seemed the whole Kingdom of Caledonia was celebrating, together with the newly wedded couple.

And as to the Prince, he simply could not stop looking adoringly into the Princess's big beautiful eyes.

THE END

Richard and Martha

A STORY ABOUT A TRUE FRIENDSHIP AND
BITTER BETRAYAL.

CHAPTER ONE

Which tells about the difficulty of growing up in a Royal Palace.

This very old and nearly forgotten story began with the birth of a baby boy. His parents, the King and Queen, named him Richard or, as they also affectionately called him, little Richie.

The King and Queen enjoyed spending all of their free time with the baby, raising the little boy within the walls of the palace. As it was often the case in royal families back then, Richie's parents never allowed him to go outside the palace to avoid possible dangers.

For the first few years, the King and Queen easily found ways to entertain their little son. However, as time passed and Richie grew to become a rebellious young boy, eventually he no longer found anything interesting in the games offered by his parents, while the absence of other children in the palace made him feel quite lonely.

One day, the little Prince was bored with yet another unexciting day, so he decided to entertain himself by hiding from his inattentive nanny. He quietly ran away from her and hid in the royal kitchen - a busy place where all the servants worked tirelessly around the clock, under the command of the Chief Maid.

Right there, among numerous hardworking cooks and chefs, Richie unexpectedly saw a little girl peeling potatoes. Judging by her dirty apron and tired look, she too was one of the kitchen workers.

Richie was so surprised to see someone of his age in such an unexpected place that he completely froze in astonishment and was not able to take his eyes off her.

When the girl noticed the Prince staring at her, she gave him a modest smile. However, at that precise moment the distressed nanny burst into the kitchen and told him off for all his "disobedience and bad manners" and then immediately dragged him away.

CHAPTER TWO

In which the Little Prince finds an unexpected friendship.

Despite the nanny's considerable annoyance with the boy's misbehaviour, the little Prince was nevertheless determined to eventually sneak back into the royal kitchen to see the girl again.

As Richie found out later, the name of the little girl was Martha, and she was the daughter of the Chief Maid.

Martha spent nearly all her time in the kitchen where she was constantly helping her mother with various duties as well as practising her cookery skills in spare time.

The children quickly became good friends and Richie was very happy to finally have someone he could play with.

At first, the King and Queen kept telling Richie off for running away and spending so much time with "the kitchen girl". However, the little Prince did not take much notice of his parents' complaints and kept on playing with Martha whenever he could.

The Queen eventually decided that it was best to dismiss the Chief Maid and her little daughter. She strongly believed that the new friendship could badly taint her son's excellent royal upbringing and education.

The King was strongly against this idea and for a very practical reason: His Majesty had a true weakness for delicious food and knew that all his favourite dishes and desserts were personally prepared by the Chief Maid herself.

So, the King simply refused to accept the idea, despite the Queen's attempts to persuade him otherwise.

Eventually, as it is often the case with children, Richie's persistence prevailed and, after a while, his parents had no other choice but to accept the fact that their son continued playing with the daughter of the Chief Maid.

Inevitably, the friendship of the young Prince and Martha grew stronger and stronger day by day.

They constantly spent time together playing all sorts of games around the Palace, doing puzzles and playing board games or just simply warming their toes by the fireplace on colder winter days.

One could say with confidence that at that time there was no friendship stronger than theirs. They had no secrets between them, so much so that one day Martha revealed to Richie an important secret about her mother.

"I have something to tell you... You see, my mom is not just the Chief Maid; she is also a true healer who can predict the future and has knowledge of some of nature's biggest secrets. But above all, for the preparation of the royal dishes, she ALWAYS uses secret herbs and ingredients which she collects - before sunrise, in the nearby dark forest - in order to add truly magical flavours to everything she cooks. This is exactly why your dad loves ALL her cooking SO much!"

"Hmm... Secret herbs, you say. Predict the future, you say. So, your mother is a witch!" exclaimed the Prince pretending shock.

"Don't be a silly potato! Of course, she is NOT a witch," responded Martha with a smile. "She always uses her secret knowledge for only good deeds. My mom teaches me everything she knows, so one day I may even become a true healer myself."

"Oh, no! Under the disguise of a cute little girl hides a terrible mean witch!" shouted Richie, pulling a horrified face that only made Martha laugh even harder.

In turn, the Prince decided to reveal to Martha a long-hidden secret of his family.

"I too have a secret to share," he whispered, glancing carefully around him to make sure that no one was listening. "My parents do NOT possess any special powers, and they are the King and Queen only by the great accident of their birth!"

That revelation made them laugh so loudly that that evening that they were probably heard in all parts of the Royal Palace...

CHAPTER THREE

In which there is no place for parental understanding.

Inevitably, years passed on, one after another, and Martha gradually turned into a beautiful young woman, while Richie (or Richard as he now preferred to be called), became a stately and confident young man.

It is not surprising that over the years their friendship gradually became something much greater, and at some point they felt that they were in love with each other.

When one day the Prince told his parents about his intention to get married, the King and Queen were at first pleased and delighted.

However, when the Prince revealed that he had chosen the daughter of the Chief Maid as his bride, both parents were completely bewildered.

"It's quite obvious that the daughter of the Chief Maid cannot be a wife to the future King!" yelled his father with great annoyance. "You ought to understand that your wife MUST be of royal descent, otherwise we will become a laughing stock!"

Despite Richard's objections and his attempts to explain that true love has no boundaries, the King and Queen were determined to make him at least acquainted with a real Princess.

"According to rumours, the Princess who lives in the neighbouring Kingdom has good manners and a proper education. You MUST at least meet her, before discussing anything else!" pleaded the Queen.

After some considerable persuasion, the Prince, eventually, agreed to meet the Princess, but only to put an end to the matter, once and for all.

A few days later it was announced that the Princess had accepted the official invitation to visit the Kingdom of Caledonia. Her forthcoming visit was a huge occasion and it seemed that people from all corners of the Kingdom were ready to travel to the Royal Palace just to have a glimpse of the visiting Princess and her magnificent retinue.

Before meeting the Princess, Richard was sceptical of the whole idea. However, after their first meeting, he was without a doubt left rather impressed.

It had nothing to do with the Princess's good looks or noble education. It was her independence and honesty that struck him hard.

When they met the very first time, she was polite but kept to herself. It was obvious that she did not seek the Prince's trust or attention. Somehow it even felt as if it was the Princess who did a great favour by coming over to meet the Prince.

After the official, pompous introductions and meals, they were finally left alone to talk. At some point during their long conversation the Princess shared with great sadness that she had once been in love with a commoner and that when her parents had found out about her feelings, they had done everything in their power to stop them from seeing each other again.

After finishing her heartbreaking story, she lowered her eyes in an attempt to hide bitter tears.

This probably was the moment that made the Prince realise how surprisingly similar their lives were.

Although, at first he did not plan to see the Princess again after their first meeting, destiny decided its own way. It turned out that they had much more in common than they had anticipated.

In the end, it seemed they could not get enough of their time together sharing with each other their worries and hopes. It came about that the Princess stayed at the Royal Palace for much longer than initially intended.

CHAPTER FOUR
In which Richard breaks Martha's heart into thousands of pieces.

Martha felt huge sadness that the arrival and continued stay of the Princess had greatly changed her relationship with Richard, whom by then, she had not seen for many days. Her love for the Prince was so strong that she continued to believe that all their difficulties were temporary and that they were destined to remain together after all.

Sadly, her hopes were shattered one rainy night when Richard came down to the kitchen after many days' absence. Martha was so happy to see her beloved yet again. She ran up to him to give an affectionate hug, but he stopped her abruptly. The Prince looked anxious and avoided looking at Martha.

"We have known each other for many years." he began in a quiet voice. "It is hard for me to find the right words... but, I think you probably already know that I have fallen in love with the Princess. In all honesty, I did not expect that everything would end this way, but I hope that we can remain good friends."

These words made Martha's heart beat fast, and tears appeared in her eyes.

"But you said you loved me," she whispered.

"The truth is that since our childhood we have had no

other option but to be with each other. I have thought a lot about this lately and have come to the conclusion that we fell in love with each other simply because there was no other choice. It seems that when one does not have what one loves then one is left with no choice but love whatever one has." responded the Prince looking away.

Martha felt betrayed. Unable to control her feelings, she shouted in despair:

"But can't you see that your parents have arranged all this in order to destroy our love?!"

"This is not true," responded the Prince quietly.

"For heaven's sake, you have only known her for a few days! It is impossible to feel true love for anybody in such a short time!"

The Prince was quiet and just stood in front of Martha with his head bowed. He was about to leave but stopped short.

"You may well be right that I don't quite understand

what really is going on. Yes, I have known her for just several days. Well then, probably my love is indeed blind! All I know is that I'm happy with her, and there is nothing I can do about it!"

The Prince went away leaving heartbroken Martha behind, all by her own in the same place, where he had met her the first time many years before.

CHAPTER FIVE

In which Martha's heart is wounded so deeply that even her mother's predictions about a happier future do not comfort her.

Martha grieved as never before in her life. She had the feeling that her life no longer had any purpose without the Prince.

"Darling, someday you will understand that all this is not as tragic as it probably feels right now." said the Chief Maid, trying to comfort her daughter.

"But Mom, he promised me that he would always love me!"

"I know, darling, I know. But you are still so young," she sighed and then continued with a much lower voice. "You know, let me tell you something. I have looked in to see the predictions of the red crystal ball and have seen visions of your true love who is yet to appear in your life, sometime in the future."

"Mom, how can you say that?" exclaimed Martha with tears in her eyes. "I only love Richard, and I don't want to wait for someone else to appear!"

"Trust me, darling, from what I saw you don't even have to wait. The crystal ball's visions showed me that your true love will appear in your life as if out of nowhere when it's the right time..."

"When it's the right time! Mom, I just don't understand you! I love Richard with ALL MY HEART!"

"And you still love the Prince even though he has betrayed you?"

Martha didn't answer the question and with tears in her eyes ran out of sight. She was undoubtedly distressed and did not know what to do next. Lying in the bed in her small and modest room, Martha was crying her eyes out when suddenly her attention was distracted by cheerful sounds coming from the royal garden outside the window.

She came up to the window and moved the curtains slightly aside and to her dismay, she saw the Prince and Princess in the distance walking hand in hand alongside beautifully trimmed red rose bushes. From time to time, Richard whispered something in the Princess's ear, making her laugh happily.

Without taking her eyes off them, Martha suddenly felt hatred fill her sorrowful heart.

"Fate will punish you both." she whispered angrily through her tears, "and may destiny make you as unhappy as you have made me! If you believe that your love is blind, then I curse your love, and wish that your blind love bring you a BLIND child!"

CHAPTER SIX

In which Martha does something terrible. Something she will regret years later.

Later that day when darkness was already in charge, Martha was sitting in her barely lit room. By the dim light of a lonely burning candle, she was reading a book of curses, which she had secretly taken shortly before from her mother's modest library.

It has to be mentioned that the Chief Maid had never liked this book, but she kept it along with her other books as a vivid example of what true healers should avoid by all means.

Understandably, Martha was still very young, and there were a lot of things that would take time for her to understand. However, back then her heart was so deeply wounded that it would be a long time before she realized that sooner or later a bird of hope eventually flies out of any ashes.

That night, Martha was completely affected by feelings of jealousy, anger and desperation. Not quite understanding what she was doing, she attempted to spell a curse on the love of the Prince and his beloved Princess.

A few days after these events, the King and Queen were unexpectedly informed that the Chief Maid and her daughter had left the royal palace.

All that was known about them was that for some reason they had made a decision to move away and live somewhere in a dark forest on the edge of the Kingdom.

The Prince certainly knew the true reason why they had left the palace.

Whilst he was still completely overcome by his enormous love for the Princess, at the same time, deep down, he was very sorry for hurting Martha and for the fact that fate had played out in such a sad and unpredictable way.

Eventually, to the utter joy of the King and Queen, the Prince and Princess announced their intention to marry.

One year later the whole Kingdom celebrated the birth of their first child. The royal baby boy was lovingly named Elliott, and his devoted parents seemed to be the happiest parents on earth.

THE END

In Pursuit of Happiness

A STORY THAT PROVES THAT HAPPINESS CAN APPEAR LITERALLY FROM ANYWHERE.

CHAPTER ONE

Which makes it clear that crime is often followed by punishment.

This extraordinary story begins with the sight of a lonely woman walking across the beautiful green hills of the Caledonia Kingdom, over which dark thunderclouds hang ready to burst with heavy rain any time soon.

The woman is walking at a fast pace, with the intention to forever leave the Kingdom in which she has lived all her life and try to find happiness elsewhere.

Probably, nothing would have made this scene worthy of the reader's attention if it were not for the fact that an ambush awaited her ahead. Ten royal guards were hiding behind an old oak tree nearby. They were waiting patiently for the woman to reach the right place, and it was clear from the expression on their faces that seizing her was a matter of extreme importance.

At a precise moment, following the command of their Captain, the guardsmen jumped out of their hiding place and with all might ran towards the unsuspecting woman.

"Catch her! Don't let her go!" shouted the men to one another.

Seeing the guardsmen running fast towards her, the woman immediately turned around and ran in the opposite direction, but unsurprisingly was quickly overtaken. One of the fastest running guardsmen jumped and grabbed her leg; the woman fell onto the ground.

"Let me go!" she shouted wriggling and trying to break free, but it fast became clear that escape was not possible.

One of the men approached the restrained woman, and still breathing heavily after the chase, addressed her:

"I am the Captain of the Royal Guards. I believe your name is Martha, isn't it?"

He then took an official document out of his pocket and read it aloud.

"You are now under arrest, by the order of His Majesty the King, for the crime committed against Prince Elliott. You are accused of witchcraft, for which you will be tried and punished accordingly."

The woman lowered her head in misery. The time had come to pay for everything, she thought to herself.

"What will happen to me?" she asked in despair.

"We'll now wait for a cage-wagon to arrive shortly, and then we'll transport you to the Court of Justice. The King was furious when ordering to capture you. So, at best, you will be jailed for life; at worst... executed."

The Captain's last words drowned in the sounds of thunder shaking the dark sky above their heads. But even without hearing them, Martha knew exactly what fate awaited her ahead. She closed her eyes and raised her head towards the raindrops falling from the sky...

CHAPTER TWO

Which describes a truly extraordinary occurrence.

While the cage-wagon carrying the new prisoner slowly swayed its way along a muddy and hard-to-pass country road, Martha was deep in her miserable thoughts.

The royal guards were strolling alongside, cheerfully talking to one another. They did not anticipate that their smugly celebratory conversation was not destined to last for long, as suddenly, to everybody's surprise, the horse pulling the cage-wagon abruptly stopped. As if scared of something ahead, the animal simply refused to move forward. Vigorously shaking its head it reared up almost causing its rider to fall off.

The guardsmen were completely puzzled by the animal's

strange and unexpected behaviour and tried to calm it down until their attention was distracted by a sudden gust of wind which seemed to blow from all directions at once. Then in front of them, right above the road, as if out of nowhere, appeared a tiny circle filled with bright light and some white smoke emerging from it.

To everyone's astonishment, the circle was gradually growing larger and larger. When it was big enough, something resembling a human being in an animal skin, fell out of it, directly onto the muddy wet road underneath, followed by a large wooden club that landed right on the creature's head, making it groan in pain.

The guardsmen looked at the baffling occurrence both in awe and horror. The bright circle then began gradually shrinking until it completely disappeared, whilst the wind suddenly ceased, as if it had not blown at all.

Meanwhile, the creature that fell onto the ground attempted to stand up on its feet, but the slippery and muddy ground immediately pulled the creature back face down into the mud, making it groan even louder.

"It's the Devil himself!" shouted one of the guards immediately running away without looking back even once.

Less than a few seconds later, the rider quickly unhitched his horse from the cage-wagon and immediately galloped away, leaving no choice for the remaining guardsmen but to dash off in different directions.

Their captive, who had been observing the events from the discomfort of her cage, was completely terrified herself and cried for help, pleading for someone to open the cage door.

However, none of the fast-fleeing and terrified royal guards would even dare return for her. So, Martha had no choice but to continue observing, through the rain and the iron bars of her cage, the events unfolding right in front of her eyes.

"Aghh, it hurts!" the creature still sitting down in the middle of the road groaned again, in a human voice, "God damn it! Aghhh..!"

When the creature turned around and revealed for the

first time its mud-smeared face, Martha became convinced that under the animal skin there was indeed a man.

After several attempts, the man finally managed to slowly stand up on his feet, leaning on the club for much needed support. He kept looking around, peering into the distance, as if trying to recognise the scenery around him.

With heavy breathing and eyes wide open, his muddy face looked like that of a savage. At some point, he noticed someone in the cage-wagon and made several steps towards it.

"Stay away!" screamed Martha. "I'm armed and dangerous!"

After a slight pause, the man threw his club aside, made a couple of more steps towards the wagon and then asked:

"What year is it?"

This completely unexpected question made Martha doubt the sanity of the man in front of her.

"I'm ARMED... I'm DANGEROUS!" she repeated again much louder, though less convincingly.

"What year IS IT?" insisted the man.

Martha decided that it was best to answer rather than make the already unpredictable situation even worse.

"It is 1587 A.D."

"WHAT!" shouted the man in disbelief.

"Fifteen eighty-seven Anno Domini" Martha repeated much slower.

The man shook his head and then began muttering with frustration something about him having been deceived, and that the world was full of crooks. He then angrily kicked a fairly large stone lying on the ground and walked off limping in a random direction.

When Martha saw the man leave, she at first felt relieved but then quickly realised that without his help she would not be able to get out of the cage. Therefore, without a second thought, she shouted at the top of her voice:

"Hey! Please help me get out of this cage!"

Having made a few more steps, the man stopped. He turned around, looked at the cage, and then, rolling his eyes, headed back towards the wagon. He pulled the rusty metal door forcefully a couple of times and then paused.

"I think it is locked ..." he said thoughtfully.

"I am QUITE aware of that!" snapped Martha back with irritation.

However, the man simply ignored her answer. He quickly picked up his wooden club from the ground and hit the old metal padlock with all his might, breaking it with the first blow...

CHAPTER THREE

In which it becomes quite clear that Martha and the man in an animal skin are heading in opposite directions.

Thus, Martha unexpectedly found herself in the company of a man who, for some reason, was wearing animal skin and carrying a club in his hand. Slowly following him along the muddy road, she glanced at him occasionally with a great deal of confusion.

On one hand, Martha was grateful to her unexpected saviour, however, on the other, the uncertainty of the situation raised many questions in her head not least: "Who IS this person, and what does everything I have witnessed earlier, mean?"

Meanwhile, the man himself stopped from time to time and peered through the rain around him, shaking his head and muttering something to himself frustratedly. Having chosen the most suitable moment, Martha decided to talk to her somewhat strange companion.

"Excuse me, but where you are heading?"

The question probably caught the man by surprise, but he pulled his thoughts together and threw his hands up in the air before answering:

"I... I need suitable clothes and ... I'm going to the nearest town," he responded, pointing in the direction of a small settlement somewhere in the distance.

"I'm definitely NOT going there!" said Martha stopping. "It's just a village anyway, looks too small for a town, but even then, there could be royal guards looking for me there."

The man just shrugged his shoulders, nodded goodbye, turned around and slowly continued his way up the road.

Martha, in turn, walked in the opposite direction. Although she did not expect that the run-away guards would come back for her any time soon, she nevertheless decided to walk along the edge of the nearby forest since it could provide her with emergency shelter, if needed.

CHAPTER FOUR

In which Martha's life is hanging by a thread.

Shortly after the travellers parted, the man in an animal skin continued to slowly make his way along the road, carefully avoiding muddy rain puddles in his path.

He was muttering about something angrily when he heard a distant cry for help behind him.

He immediately turned around and peered into the distance, trying to see through the rain where it was coming from. After watching carefully and waiting a few more seconds to no avail, he was about to continue on his way when he again heard somebody scream anxiously, this time even louder.

The man somewhat overdramatically rolled his eyes and then ran in the direction of the distressed call.

He quickly reached a forest clearing where he saw Martha in the distance. She was vigorously swinging a large branch, trying to drive away a grinning wolf that was preparing to attack.

The predator was slowly approaching the frightened woman but then suddenly stopped. The wolf's ears pricked up, and it turned its head in the direction of the man running towards them.

Having caught the scary sight of the angry wolf, the man suddenly halted. He stood there as if trying to catch his breath.

"Please help me!" begged Martha at the top of her voice.

"Yes... yes... of coooourse!" shouted the man back, rolling his eyes again. "Just making a minor adjustment to this VERY uncomfortable skin!"

After an awkward adjustment to the animal skin, which seemingly puzzled Martha and further distracted the wolf, the man yelled loudly and then, like a madman, waving his club in all directions, ran at full speed towards the wolf.

The animal was determined to attack the unwanted guest, however, fell short of any action when the wooden club's unstoppable blow threw it a considerable distance away.

The man, his eyes bulging with the effort, continued to roar, swinging his club from side to side even though the predator was already fleeing the scene with its tail between its legs.

When the danger was no longer present, the man finally lowered his club breathing heavily. Martha ran up to her saviour and without saying anything at all started weeping bitterly on his shoulder.

CHAPTER FIVE

Which finally reveals the name of the man in animal skin.

"I cannot thank you enough! If it wasn't for you then my encounter with the wolf would have ended terribly," said Martha with a tremble in her voice yet mindful to adjust her shaggy hair.

The man nodded modestly, hoping that his blushing cheeks were not visible under the dirt on his face.

"And who would have thought," continued Martha with a smile, "that although we met just a short while ago, you have already saved my life twice!"

The man smiled uneasily - he was not quite used to the role of a hero.

"I am Charlie, by the way," he introduced himself, stretching out his dirty hand.

"I am Martha," she responded with a smile, shaking his hand.

Charlie was patiently waiting for Martha, who was tidying herself up after the stressful incident when at some point his attention was distracted by a red ball which Martha had briefly taken out from the small leather bag on her belt.

"That's unexpected," he said staring at it. "I am seeing this ball for the second time today."

Martha paused for a second and then shook her head thoughtfully.

"This fortune ball is unique, and it has some very special qualities. You see, whoever can interpret it, can also predict the future. Many years ago I got it from my mother. No one knows anything about its origins. However, one thing I am certain about, is that you could not have seen it elsewhere as it is the only one, and I always carry it with me."

"That may well be true." responded Charlie, "it's just that the ball I saw earlier was the same colour, same size and had that same number eight carved on top of it."

"Well, it is not a number." corrected him Martha, "It is a symbol: a symbol of infinity."

Charlie looked into the distance thoughtfully and then, after a pause, responded hesitantly.

"I know that what I am about to tell you will sound unbelievable but... I come from the future. Indeed, from a rather distant future. I travelled in time with the help of I.M.C..."

"I.M.C?" repeated Martha.

"Yes, it stands for Interdimensional Molecular Catapult. It is a special invention that allows you to travel in time, I am quite sure that I saw a similar ball shortly before my journey."

Martha gave a rather sceptical look at her companion before voicing her doubts.

"Even though the animal skin you are wearing suits you well..."

"You are not the first one to point that out..." noted Charlie quickly.

"Yet," she continued, "there's no way you look like someone from a distant future..."

Charlie just sighed heavily, as he knew perfectly what she meant.

CHAPTER SIX

In which Charlie tells Martha about life in the future.

As time passed, Charlie became noticeably cheerful. He had a feeling that many days had passed since the moment he travelled in time. In just one day he had experienced more than in all of his previous life. He felt as though he was living the life of a completely different person.

The travellers rambled slowly across fields talking about all sorts of things, and it was obvious that they were quite enjoying each other's company.

"By the way, I was wondering about that fortune ball of yours." said Charlie thoughtfully, "Have you seen what the future holds for you?"

"No, I have not and do not intend to. Seeing your own future would be a big mistake. Life would then become a constant wait for happy moments and endless fearful anticipating of unhappy ones. And I guess, one does not need a fortune ball to realise that sooner or later everything comes to an end," summed up Martha with sadness in her voice. "What about the times where you come from? What does the future look like?"

Charlie was about to reply but then paused. Of course, he had a lot to tell Martha about all the amazing inventions of the future. However, he suddenly realised that he would never be able to reproduce any of them. And since he had always been just a consumer, the inventions of the future were now as unattainable to him as they were to Martha.

"Well, let's put it this way, in the future people buy all sorts of things, most of which they do not even need.

"Well, that's somewhat I witness every time I visit the town market. Not much will change then..." frowned Martha with a wry smile.

CHAPTER SEVEN

In which Martha and Charlie find themselves at a crossroads where they part to never meet again.

After a long passage, the travellers eventually joined a narrow rural road. They had enjoyed their conversation along the way and were somewhat saddened when realised that the road had brought them to a crossroads.

An old mossy post right in front of them informed that the road to the left led to the "Neighbouring Kingdom", while the road to the right led to the "Nearest Town".

Standing at the crossroads, the travellers were deep in their own thoughts, and Martha was the first to break the uneasy silence.

"I simply cannot thank you enough for all of your help and interesting company! But, I guess it is time to part.

Charlie lowered his eyes and then nodded in silence.

"Take care, and please do not tell every passer-by that you are from the future," said Martha with a smile.

They shook hands and then gave each other an awkward hug. They both had a strange feeling that they had known each other for a very long time.

"Farewell, Charlie!"

"Farewell, Martha!"

And so they walked off in different directions - Martha towards the neighbouring Kingdom while Charlie headed towards the nearest town.

However, it was no wonder that every step they took away from each other became harder and harder.

At some point, they both stopped as if some invisible force would not let them part. They turned and caught each other's glance. Then, first hesitantly, but then faster and faster, they ran towards each other and hugged affectionately.

"Martha," exclaimed Charlie looking straight into her eyes, "at first I thought that the whole time travel thing was just a big mistake and that the time machine thingy..."

"You mean I.M.C..." Martha smiled knowingly.

"Yes, ...that the I.M.C. thingy had got everything completely wrong. But now I feel that everything that has happened to me - happened for a reason!"

"You know," said Martha looking straight into his eyes, "many years ago my mother told me that someone worthy would appear in my life out of nowhere when the right time came. I have just realised exactly what she meant... You have appeared in my life, literally out of nowhere, when I least expected you!"

And so, they stood talking to each other until Charlie said the most important words of his life.

"I do not want to leave you!"

"But didn't you want to get some clothes from the town?" she teased.

"What I am wearing will do just fine for now!"

Martha smiled and then said thoughtfully:

"You know, somehow I believe that one can draw conclusions from any story."

"So, what conclusion would you draw from ours?" asked Charlie with interest.

She looked thoughtfully far into the direction from which the cold autumn wind was blowing.

"Well, perhaps it is not only fairytales that end well," said Martha with a smile.

"Having said that," she continued somewhat seriously, "don't you think that this story is getting slightly too cheesy and may well turn out like most textbook love stories?"

Charlie nodded struggling to hold back a smile and then, he took her hand, tightly gripped the club in his other hand, and shouted at the top of his voice:

"Let's ruuuun!"

And they both ran off, holding hands and laughing all the way, sprinting between the two roads through the endless green field which had no end in sight...

THE END

ACKNOWLEDGEMENTS

This book would not have been possible without the kind help and assistance of Pauline Chernilovskaya, The Safin Family and Louise Swann.

Printed in Great Britain
by Amazon

23053904R00074